Hey, God! What Does "Different" Mean?

Roxie Cawood Gibson
Printed and Illustrated by Jim Gibson

Isbn:0-9763134-4-8

For nearly 50 years, Roxie Gibson has poured her heart and soul into caring for young people. As our Head Angel at Oak Hill School, she reflects God's love in her gentle words, warm hugs, and with her wonderful books which speak to all children at any age. In *Hey, God! What Does "Different" Mean?*, Ms. Roxie reminds all of us that we are special and "especially important and loved." A perfect and timely message. In Matthew 18, Jesus instructs his disciples to become like a child. Roxie holds a child's heart close to her own, and her writing gives us a special insight into the innocence and beauty of children. Ms. Roxie has been a gift to me, and like her other books, *Hey, God! What Does "Different" Mean?* will be a gift for years to come.

Hart Roper, Head of Oak Hill School

Nashville, Tennessee

*This book is dedicated
with utmost love to our
Lord and Savior Jesus Christ,
and to Michael, Joey and
children everywhere who are
"different".*

Hey, God, I'm really glad You stay awake at night so I can talk with You!

Sometimes
when I wake
up and it's
dark, I'm a
little lonesome

and
scared.

-3-

I love talking
with You, God.

You make me
feel so safe,
and You are
so smart!

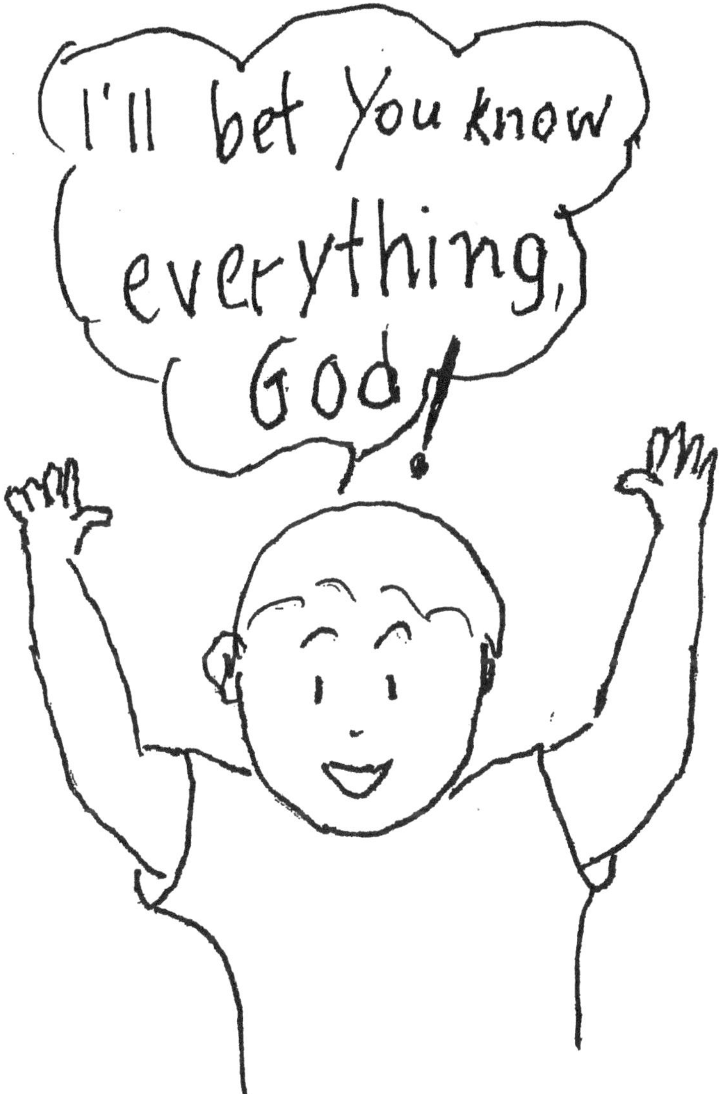
I'll bet You know everything, God!

You alway know
the answer to
my questions,
God. My Mom
tries, but
sometimes
my questions
are too hard
  for her

You see, God
today we were in
the grocery store
and a boy looked
at me and
giggled.
His Mom told

him that I
was "different"
and that he
shouldn't stare

This happens
pretty often,
God, so I asked
my Mom what
"Different"
means.

She had
tears in her
eyes as she
hugged me
and said we
would talk
about it
later.

I didn't want
to make Mom
sad (You know I
love her so much),
So I decided to

Google mister
Webster to
find the answer.

Different
unlike
unique
distinct

Ample

He said that
"different"
means
unlike,
~~unik~~
unique,
or distinct.

different

unlike   distinct

unique

-18-

now that
sounds pretty
good, but I
thought I
heard you
whisper in
my ear,
"Different
means
Special."

-19-

And I know
what "special"
means, God.

It means
especially
important

and
loved!

Thank You, God,
for making me
special!

That means
I am loved
and I can
love everyone!

The next time
Someone calls
me "Different,"
I'll smile at
them because
I know I'm
Special!

Me

And thank
You, God, for
my sweet
family that
always knew

I was

special!

But, most of all, thank you for loving me....

I love You too, God!

OTHER BOOKS BY ROXIE CAWOOD GIBSON

HEY, GOD! LISTEN!
HEY, GOD! WHERE ARE YOU?
HEY, GOD! WHAT IS CHRISTMAS?
HEY, GOD! HURRY!
HEY, GOD! WHAT IS AMERICA?
HEY, GOD! WHAT IS DEATH?
HEY, GOD! WHAT IS TERRORISM?
HEY, GOD! WHAT MAKES YOU HAPPY?
HEY, GOD! WHAT IS COMMUNION?
HEY, GOD! WHAT IS BAPTISM?
HEY, GOD! WHAT IF....?

TWO LITTLE FISHES AND FIVE LOAVES OF BREAD
JUST ME, LORD
DO RAGWEEDS BLOOM?
WAYS TO BE HAPPY
ON GRANDMA'S MOUNTAIN
TALKING WITH GOD
HERE HE IS

MUSICALS

HEY, GOD! LISTEN!
HEY, GOD! WHAT IS CHRISTMAS?
HEY, GOD! HURRY!
HEY, GOD! WHAT IS AMERICA?

Printed in the USA
CPSIA information can be obtained
at www.ICGtesting.com
LVHW051436180224
772154LV00008B/101

9 780976 313441